PUFFIN BOOKS

The Dressed-up Giant

Other titles in the First Young Puffin series

The Dressed-up Giant

Kaye Umansky

Illustrated by
Doffy Weir

PUFFIN BOOKS

PUFFIN BOOKS

Published by the Penguin Group
Penguin Books Ltd, 80 Strand, London,WC2R 0RL, England
Penguin Putnam Inc., 375 Hudson Street, New York, New York 10014, USA
Penguin Books Australia Ltd, Ringwood,Victoria, Australia
Penguin Books Canada Ltd, 10 Alcorn Avenue,Toronto, Ontario, Canada M4V 3B2
Penguin Books India (P) Ltd, 11 Community Centre, Panchsheel Park, New Dehli – 110 0117, India
Penguin Books (NZ) Ltd, Cnr Rosedale and Airborne Roads, Albany, Auckland, New Zealand
Penguin Books (South Africa) (Pty) Ltd, 5 Watkins Street, Denver Ext 4, Johannesburg 2094, South Africa

On the World Wide Web at: www.penguin.com

Penguin Books Ltd, Registered Offices: Harmondsworth, Middlesex, England

First published, 2001
3 5 7 9 10 8 6 4

Text copyright © Kaye Umansky, 2001
Illustrations copyright © Doffy Weir, 2001
All rights reserved

The moral right of the author and illustrator has been asserted

Set in Bembo Schoolbook

Printed in Hong Kong by Midas Printing Ltd

British Library Cataloguing in Publication Data
A CIP catalogue record for this book is available from the British Library

ISBN 0–141–30479–0

Giant Waldo
was eating his
breakfast when
Heavy Hetty came
running in excitedly
from the cave next door.

"Waldo, guess what?" she gasped.
"Beefy Betty and Ed are getting
married and we've been invited to the
wedding!"

"Great," said Waldo. Well, it was. Beefy Betty was Hetty's best friend. They often wrestled together. Ed was their coach. He had flashing white teeth and big, bulging muscles.

"I've got nothing to wear," announced Hetty. "There's a new store just opened in town called Whopping Shopping. I'll go there."

"What's wrong with what you're wearing?" asked Waldo.

"I can't wear *wrestling* gear to a *wedding*, silly!"

"What, we've got to get all dressed up, have we?" said Waldo doubtfully. He wasn't keen on dressing up.

"Of course! You'll need a suit."

"I've got one," said Waldo, brightening up. "I had it for my birthday."

"Which birthday?" asked Hetty suspiciously.

"My twelfth, I think. Why?"

"Try it on," ordered Hetty.

So Waldo went and tried on the suit. It was mud-brown. The jacket was very tight under the arms and the buttons wouldn't do up. The trousers ended at his knees. On top of the wardrobe he found an old top hat which had belonged to his grandfather. He put it on and looked at himself in the mirror.

"That'll do," said Waldo. "I look fine in this suit." And he went to show Hetty.

"It's too small," said Hetty.

"It's fine," said Waldo.

"It's too *small*," insisted Hetty. "And it's a horrible colour and very old-fashioned. I'm not going to the wedding with you wearing that. Come on. We're going shopping."

So they set off to Giant Town to visit Whopping Shopping.

Hetty bought new shoes, a dress, a
handbag and a wonderful hat with
flowers on. She took *ages*. Waldo just
hung around yawning.

"Right," said Hetty. "That's me
finished. Now for your suit."

"I'd like a mud-brown one,"
Waldo told the assistant.

"No, he wouldn't," said Hetty.
"He'd like something bright and
colourful."

"Mud-brown *suits* me," protested
Waldo. "You know where you are
with mud."

But Hetty wouldn't hear of it. So,
reluctantly, Waldo began trying on
suits.

He tried on a pink
suit, but he didn't
like the colour.

He tried on a
green suit, but he
didn't like the
buttons.

He tried on a blue
suit, but he didn't
like the trousers.

Finally, Hetty came racing
up with a buttercup-yellow suit.

Waldo didn't like the colour, the
buttons or the trousers. And he didn't
like the hat, the shirt or the tie
that Hetty chose to go
with it.

"It's horrible," said Waldo.
"Nonsense," said Hetty firmly. "It's
perfect. I'm going to feel so proud of
you at the wedding. Now let's go and
get you some new shoes."

"New *shoes*?" shrieked Waldo.
"What's wrong with my old boots?
Years of wear left in these . . ."

"You're having new shoes and a
haircut. Then we'll decide on a
wedding present. What do you think?
Towels, teapot or toaster?"

On the morning
of the wedding,
Waldo dragged
himself over to
the wardrobe
and reluctantly
put on his dazzling
new outfit.

"Everyone will
laugh at me," he
thought gloomily.
"I'll stick out like
a sore thumb."

He sighed, straightened his hateful new tie and hat and stepped out from the cave in his squeaky new shoes.

In the cave next door, Hetty stood before *her* mirror.

"Although I say it myself," said Hetty, "I look pretty good." And she patted her flowery hat, picked up her new handbag and the gift-wrapped toaster and went out to meet Waldo.

"Oh, Waldo! You look so smart!"
she cried when she saw him. "What a
difference it makes when you're all
dressed up."

"Mmm," said Waldo.
He forced a smile
on his face.

Hetty was looking so happy,
he didn't want to spoil things.
"The hat looks great, Het. Do you
water it regularly?"

"Silly," giggled Hetty. And she put a
flower in his buttonhole, tucked her
arm into his and together they set off
down the mountain.

It was a very blustery day.
They hadn't gone far when a
huge gust of wind blew Hetty's
hat high into the air.

"My hat!" wailed Hetty. "Oh,
Waldo! My lovely hat!"

"Stay there, Het!" shouted Waldo
gallantly. "I'll get it!"

The hat blew down into a steep ravine. Waldo bounded after it, shoes skidding on the loose rocks. He had almost reached it when . . .

. . . it flew off again, into some brambles. Boldly, Waldo thrust his way in amongst the thorns.

"Mind out for your suit!" cried Hetty.

The hat blew out of the brambles
and into a tree, where it sat at the end
of a very long, thin branch. Waldo
climbed the tree and bravely crawled
out along the branch. But the hat
flipped away just before he could
touch it.

"Your suit!"
screamed Hetty as
he backtracked
along the branch.
"Be careful of your
suuuuuit!"

But Waldo was
down, off and
running again.
Towards the river
this time.

"Waldo!" howled
Hetty. "Roll up
your trousers!"

But Waldo was already wading into
the river, where Hetty's hat sat on a
rock, right in the middle.

This time he was
successful.

"Here!" he gasped, puffing up the slope. "I got it, Het. It looks fine."

"Thank you, Waldo," said Hetty. "I only wish I could say the same about you."

"Oh dear," said Waldo. His triumphant smile faded. "I'm in a bit of a mess, aren't I?"

He was. His shoes were ruined. His
trousers were soaked. His jacket was
covered in green moss stains. His shirt
was torn, his tie was wonky and he
had lost his hat.

He looked up at Hetty. Her
shoulders were shaking. She was
holding a hanky to her eyes.

"Sorry," he said. "I didn't mean to let you down. Don't cry, Het."

"I'm not," said Hetty. "I'm laughing."

And she was. Tears were streaming down her face. "Oh, Waldo. You look so funny!"

"I know," said Waldo, with a sheepish grin. Then he started to laugh too. They couldn't stop for ages.

"Come on," said Hetty, finally. "We'd better go and get you changed or we'll be *really* late."

"Lucky I've still got my old suit," said Waldo. And, still giggling, they hurried back up the mountain.

They got to the wedding just as the
bells rang out. Beefy Betty and Ed
stood on the steps, holding hands and
smiling. Betty wore a big white dress
which matched Ed's teeth.

Lots of gigantic friends and relations
threw confetti and clicked cameras.
The women were all decked out in
flowery dresses and hats. As for the
men . . .

"They're all wearing too-tight suits!" said Waldo as they joined the cheering crowd. "You see? I look just right. Don't I?"

"Well . . . put it this way. You look like you," said Hetty, smiling up at him. "And that's fine by me," she added.

Then, much to his surprise, she gave him a hard shove.

"Out of my way!" she snapped.

On the steps, Betty drew back her muscular arm and threw her bouquet of flowers into the crowd.

Guess who caught it?